The following stories are based on true events. Based does not intend to mean they are completely true events.

Some of the content in this book may be scary. Please understand this. I would not advise reading this book at night. (Just my two cents.)

Names and places in this book have been changed in order to give it more fictional value, and to respect the privacy of others.

This book is copyrighted and shall not be reproduced in any way without the Authors consent.

All rights reserved. No part of this publication may be transmitted or reproduced in any form or by any means. This includes photocopying, electronic, mechanical, or by storage system (informational or otherwise), unless given written permission by the author.

November©2019 Ivy Evans

Dedication:

This book is dedicated to my husband. Thank you for being so supportive, I love you.

This book contains a collaboration of paranormal ghost stories based on true events.

The stories in this book are mostly events that are Hauntings where ghosts have most likely not shown themselves to the haunted, but made their prescense known in other sinister ways.

CHAPTER ONE
Always A Dreamer

My family and I moved into a house built in the early 1900's. It had been recently remodeled so not much of the original building was left.

The day my husband, my two sons and I moved in was chaotic. But what I remember most of all about that day was, when we immediately entered the front door it was freezing.

My husband had gone over to check the thermostat. It was set at sixty-eight. It did not feel sixty-eight, it felt like twenty. I shivered and headed to put some boxes in the kitchen.

My sons were running amuck, giggling and play fighting. I had to constantly tell them to be careful and knock it off. Frustrated, I had gone into the bathroom with a box of bathroom items and shut the door, trying to clear my head mostly and have a minute to myself. This move had been so stressful.

As I was running my hands under the warm water and splashing it on my face, I looked up at myself in the mirror. I looked so tired. The late nights of packing were definitely wearing on me.

I splashed some more water on my face and reached down into the box for a roll of paper towels. When I was upright again, water still dripping off my face, I saw her. A little girl standing behind me, head cocked to the side, smirking.

I froze. I wanted to wipe my face, but she looked so menacing and I was scared of blocking my vision for even a moment. Could she hurt me?

Finally, I mustered the courage to wipe the water off of my face and she was gone.

What I had hoped would be a stress relief had turned into something completely different.

I exited the bathroom, stiffly trying to gain my wits. What had just happened? Was I so sleep deprived from packing that I made it all up?

After fifteen minutes or so and nothing else unusual happening, I shrugged it off and went back to unloading the truck.

That evening, in our half-unpacked room, I laid on the mattress on the floor next to my husband. (We had not had time to put together bedframes yet.) He was exhausted and ready for sleep. I, on the other hand, needed to read first to wipe away some of the day.

We had a small table lamp plugged in a foot or so away from our mattress. I turned it on and began to read. Before long, my eyes were heavy and burning and I could not read anymore. I kept reading the same sentences over and over.

I rolled over on my side and reached to turn off the lamp. But before I reached the switch, the bulb burst. Shards of broken bulb cascaded over the back of my hand like fallen snowflakes.

I gasped and sat there terrified. What had just happened? The bulb did just fine in our old house.

I laid there for minutes just listening for anything to be afraid of. Nothing. I was too tired to clean up the bulb mess, so I wrote it off for something to take care of in the morning.

Finally, I scooted deep under the blankets and spooned up against my husband, as if his sleeping body could keep me safe. He snored on, impervious to the light bulb shattering.

Finally, I drifted off. I do not usually dream, but in this house, I dreamt all of the time. Almost every single night. And they were not good dreams, but reoccurring dreams of terror.

I dreamt I was a little girl around the age of eight. A man led me tightly by the wrist into the basement of our new house. I did not put up a fight even though the grip he had on my wrist was so tight that I worried it would bruise.

I looked up at the man, and his facial features were present, but blurred. This confused me. I somehow knew in my dream that this man was my father, but I could not see clearly enough that he was.

In the basement, there was a sink in the far corner. A small stand alone, with a deep bowl. The bowl was full to the top edges with water. The man stopped me in front of the sink and slapped me across the face so hard, I fell hard onto the ground.

Through strands of hair I gazed at him, shocked and hurt. His blurred face smirked or smiled, hard to tell which.

My body began to shake in terror. What was I to do? And why was this happening? These thoughts sprinkled my mind consistently.

Again, he grabbed my wrist and pulled me to my feet. He pulled my hair back as if putting it in a ponytail and plunged my face into the water.

I kicked at the air and screamed in muffled sobs which were absorbed by a waterless abyss. I choked on water and felt everything going black.

He pulled my head from the sink. His face was inches from mine when I heard him speak. "I will fucking kill you," he hissed. Then, before I had a moment to comprehend or run, my face was driven deep into the water. Again, I was fighting for my life. Kicking, using my hands as leverage on the sink, I tried to pull my head out, but to no avail.

As the blackness surrounded me a second time, I woke up coughing, holding my throat.

The room was pitch black. My husband's snores were barely audible next to me. I scanned the room, searching for familiarity. Reality set in, and I remembered where I was. The new house.

My heart racing, I laid there in the dark, trying to catch my breath. What a dream. What a horrid, horrid--

Footsteps. From the hallway. Stomping closer and closer to the door. They were too heavy to be my son. My heart began pulsing faster, and faster, my chest aching.

The handle of the door, which we had shut when we went to bed, jangled. Slightly...just enough to hear.

I held my breath and laid there. Do I put the covers over my head and close my eyes like a five-year-old? Do I just sit still and hope it goes away? Do I wake my husband and tell him? So many thoughts cascaded, too many to recollect. The only thought I held on to immensely was, *I am going to die.*

CHAPTER TWO
Basements Are Always Spooky

The mall was not my ideal job. I'm like any other person. Sometimes you must work a job that is only "O.K." before you get to have the job that you truly enjoy.

The mall I worked at was both an outdoor and indoor mall. Some of the eateries were on the outside for easy access to patrons, while a few were littered here and there on the inside as well.

The employees were friendly to a point. They helped me learn quite quickly and I was off doing my job in the basement.

The basement was not my favorite place to work at all. Unfortunately, I was stuck working down there for over a year.

In the basement they kept a lot of the extra merchandise for most of the stores. My job was pricing and tagging it in case they needed to do a quick restock which, around the holidays, was fairly often.

Almost on the dot daily, I would arrive at eight in the morning. I often would be sporting a sweater because it was fall. The basement was always the perfect temperature until ten in the morning.

At ten o'clock every morning, even though it was warming up outside, it would turn freezing in the basement. I always had to layer on an additional jacket and I could see my breath.   At first, that was the only odd thing, so I would just go about my job.

Then there was this radio in the corner. It was a cheap, old, eighties radio. Sometimes, I would use it for background noise while I shifted boxes around getting to more items to price. But more often than not, I would be so enthralled with the job I was doing that I would forget it even existed.

Sometimes, however, it would turn on randomly by itself. I would drop what I was doing and go over and turn it off.

I would always think to myself that I should ask management if I could throw it out, because the dang thing was glitchy. But I never did.

Another time, I was working by a table. I had out a bunch of dolls in their boxes. I had to go to the bathroom super bad. I kept looking over my shoulder as I was working because I felt like I was being watched.

Finally, when I felt like I was at a stopping point to where I could go relieve myself, I went to the bathroom.

Drying my hands off on my pants as I came back from the bathroom (because the paper towel dispenser was on the fritz again), I stopped in my tracks.

I stood there frozen in place for a few minutes. The hairs on the back of my neck stood on end, and my mouth had to be gaping open in shock.

I must have had around twenty doll boxes on that table. The boxes were ripped to shreds on the floor. The dolls were lined up perfectly next to each other on the table. Try explaining that one to your manager!

I did not get fired, but I did have to reimburse the company for each of those dolls out of my next paycheck.

At this point, everything was definitely adding up. This was not just a few "weird" things happening. Something was going on in this basement, and now it was costing me money.

Fast forward a week, maybe two. I had just put in for a department transfer after the doll incident and I was waiting, extremely hopeful that it would be approved.

A co-worker was helping me load some merchandise onto a dolly so he could bring it upstairs to one of the stores.

To our amazement, a toy truck came out from behind some boxes and started driving itself around in circles. Its siren was blaring, wa-wa, wa-wa.

He looked at me, and I looked back at him. We both got out of there as fast as we could. I sat him down upstairs on our break, explaining everything I had been going through. I was lucky he witnessed the truck incident because he helped me convince my manager to lower the cost of the dolls on my check, as well as to approve my department move.

I have not had the luxury of working in the basement for several years and never plan to again. I now work upstairs in the mall. Do I hear stories from others who have worked in the basement? Yes, all the time. And I believe every one of them.

CHAPTER THREE
Restaurant or Daycare?

I used to be a waitress. It was a job I adored. The people who came in and out were almost like family to me.

Then one year, my mother got sick. So, I moved my son and I into her house so I could help take care of her at night when her aide was gone for the day.

I ended up getting hired at a local restaurant. They were extremely flexible on hours, which really helped my situation. I jumped at the chance to take this job.

After only a few days at the new job, I started noticing some odd things. For instance, the temperature fluctuated all over the place. One minute it would be freezing, another sweltering. We would all go check the thermostat. It would read the exact same temperature every time we checked, whether it felt too hot or too cold.

Some customers would complain too, but most didn't mind, or maybe they just didn't notice it like we did.

Then, in the kitchen, when I would be putting garnishes on the plates before bringing the food out, I would hear baby cries. They were muffled and soft. But there would not be a single customer with a baby in the joint.

In the back hallway, next to the bathrooms, myself and others have also heard giggling. It was as if a little girl was giggling, but no one was there. And, although I had not personally heard this, a co-worker heard stomping footsteps, like a child playing hopscotch in the hallway by the bathrooms.

He swears there is the spirit of a little girl playing in that hallway.

The dishwasher has had multiple encounters while he was rinsing dishes. At numerous times, stacks of clean dishes have been knocked off his table and shattered on the floor. There is no door nearby for a gust of wind to do it.

The manager has been frequently annoyed with this activity. We have a dry erase board where the weekly schedule is written and, on several occasions, that board has been wiped clean, or mostly wiped.

After confronting some co-workers about some of these events I have seen and heard, I was told that the building used to operate as a daycare.

It caught on fire thirty years ago and a few children died in the fire. They think the building is being haunted by children who are either lost in this world or are having too much fun playing tricks to leave.

CHAPTER FOUR
Non-Fat, No Foam, Medium Temp Latte

I worked at a coffee shop for about ten years. Friends and co-workers would often ask me why I stayed working there as long as I did. To be honest, the weird activity occurring there did not scare me as much as it entertained me.

One day, my boss was getting freaked out because the coffee grinder would randomly turn on and off. He talked corporate into buying a new one. I think he told them it was defective or something. However, after installing the new one, it immediately started doing the same exact thing. It really shook him.

Once, when I was using the bathroom, which is back down the hall, I heard footsteps. They were loud footsteps, from a bigger individual. I opened the bathroom door, but the hallway was empty. Also, no one who worked there weighed over about a buck fifteen.

Another day, Jack, one of my fellow baristas, went in the back to grab some medium-sized paper cups because we ran out. He set them on the counter to help a customer at the register. Once he was done, he turned around and the entire stack of one hundred cups was gone. How do one hundred cups just disappear? We never found them. We had to sell mediums and larges only until our new shipment came in the following week.

The last incident I can recall was when I was working with Emilee. We were both set to open that day. We arrived about the same time, went in together, and she went to deactivate all of the alarms. I immediately went to turn on the coffee equipment.

I walked behind the counter—and just stopped cold. Something was all over the floor. It took me a few seconds to realize what the heck it was.

Every cap to every syrup bottle was off and lying on the floor. And I mean all of them! The twist cap kind too. So, whatever was haunting that place had popped off every last one of them. It was like thirty to forty caps!

My co-workers and I did talk about everything that happened here and there. The story that I've heard is that there used to be a very heavyset woman who would come in and give the baristas a hard time.

She was one of those customers who would always order a Non-Fat, Low Foam, Medium Temp-only drink. She never was a happy woman and she always found something to complain about.

One day, she got her coffee and got into an argument with one of the baristas. She walked off in quite the huff and didn't look before crossing the road. There was a screech of tires....she was hurt pretty badly.

They took her to the hospital, and she was expected to pull through. But I guess her body couldn't handle the trauma of the accident and she had a stroke and passed away.

So, everyone at the coffee shop thinks that the crazy, heavyset lady who used to yell about her coffee is taunting the baristas as payback. What do I believe? I think that someone either really hates coffee from the beyond, or they might be right.

CHAPTER FIVE
Counseling The Living or The Dead?

I began my new practice right out of school. Was so elated to have my degree and start helping others. Especially children. I had a somewhat sordid past, so this was my dream. I was committed to helping kids make it through life happier and healthier than I did.

Around the corner from my apartment was the perfect spot to open my new counseling center. There were already three other counselors practicing there and they had only one open office (which I leased).

On my first day of work, I only had a few clients because I was just starting out. I walked in excited, a little anxious and nervous.

Becky, one of the other counselors (she usually does marriage counseling), came up to me and welcomed me to the practice and shook my hand.

We gabbed for a little bit since I arrived way earlier than my first appointment. She talked about her kids and her husband. Me, being single... I talked about my cat, my favorite television shows and my area of practice.

While we were finishing up our conversation, there was this low moaning down the hall. I looked at Becky and she seemed to just shrug it off. It was really weird, but if she wasn't worried about it, I figured I could shrug it off too.

I went about my day. I started arranging my office and unpacking my briefcase with all the necessary essentials I thought to bring. I hung a few pictures on the wall, along with my degree.

When I finally sat down and checked the time, it was around nine thirty in the morning. That's when I heard it right outside of my office door. The moaning. It wasn't really loud, like a soft moan, but definitely not a happy one. It sounded pained, but again, not too audible.

Quickly, I opened my door and peered out. No one was there. I shut my office door and sat back in my chair confused. At that moment, the entire office got freezing cold. It was as if it were January, not June.

I again opened the door to my office and checked the thermostat, which was set to a decent temperature. Shrugging, I went back into my office and sat down.

My first appointment was at ten o'clock. They arrived a few minutes early, and since I was eager to start my new job, I started the session a little early.

While my client was telling me her back story and I was furiously trying to keep up with my notes, I heard a voice in my ear. "Why are you here…"

Instinctively, I turned around in my chair. No one was there, which, in hindsight, I should have realized right away (it was a one-person session).

My client paused and eyed me suspiciously like I was crazy or something. I nodded for her to continue and mumbled something about a possible fly buzzing near me.

The rest of the session went smoothly without a hitch. I walked her to the door, thanked her and told her that I would see her next week.

My next appointment was sitting in the waiting room, so I brought him back. Once I got in the office, again it was freezing. I quickly excused myself and checked the thermostat again. It was fine.

Back in the office, I sat down and began the session. I listened, took notes, and that session went absolutely fine. No weird whispers and no moans.

The next one, however, was a little weird. She was still in high school, having a hard time being bullied at school. It just broke my heart that she had suicidal thoughts just because people had to make fun of her for whatever reason.

She was explaining a situation at school where bullies slammed her into a locker and laughed at her. Then, without warning, she started screaming, "Shut up! Go away!"

It really took me off guard. I did not see signs of a multiple personality disorder or anything similar when we were talking. I noted it on my pad and acted like it hadn't affected me one bit.

She apologized and continued, a little anxiously. For about another fifteen minutes she talked, and I listened. Then she started screaming again, "I'm here to get help -- leave me alone!"

I sat there trying to act like nothing was happening. But in my mind, I was starting to get really freaked out!

After our session was over, (she was my last of the day) I met up with Becky. I asked her if she had ever experienced anything weird or heard anything unusual there. That's when she told me why my office had been vacant in the first place.

A few months ago, a counselor was seeing a client in my new office. She had worked there for five years or so. She was treating this troubled lady who creeped out everyone else in the office.

She would talk about her husband to the lady at the front desk all the time. He was deployed somewhere and she missed him all the time.

So, all Becky could assume was that she was depressed her husband was away, made tougher by the fact that she just had three-month-old twins that he hadn't even met yet. Becky assumed she had a high case of postpartum.

Anyway, I guess one day she came to counseling with a knife and stabbed her counselor to death. In... my... office. She then slit her wrists. It was a horrific murder-suicide.

They didn't find either of them until the end of the day when the secretary was locking up. She had knocked on the door to ask her if she was staying late (which is not something she normally did), and I guess that's when she found them and called the police.

So, needless to say, I started my practice in a haunted office. I asked my client what she had been hearing that made her yell. She told me a lady was whispering in her ears.

I asked her what the lady said to her. She said the first time she told her "Just end it already." And the second time she asked her "Why are you here?" Which is exactly what I heard whispered in my ear when I was alone in my office!

None of my other clients have heard whispers. I hear them from time to time and its always almost as light as the wind. So low that you wonder if it really happened.

Since those incidents, a few other have happened. Almost daily, something knocks my pen holder off of my desk and onto the floor. (It's quite annoying.)

Twice, I've come in from my lunch break and found all the papers that were on my desk scattered on the floor. It was as if someone had opened a window and a gust of wind had strewn them about. But all my windows were all shut and locked, I checked.

Occasionally, there's a random "shushing." It's almost like a spirit thinks this is a library or something. I thought maybe it was her trying to shush everyone so that her whispers could be heard, I don't know.

It's definitely creepy. I'm hoping to have enough saved from my practice soon to be able to open an office in a better location… one that isn't haunted.

CHAPTER SIX
Paranormal Massages

The first unusual happening that I noticed at the spa did not quite spell out H-A-U-N-T-E-D by any means. I viewed it as a subtle build to what was to come.

Chloe and I were starting a couple's massage in the far back room. We always begin our massages by stretching out muscles and rubbing them. Next, we get the essential oils out. We have our clients smell them and take deep relaxing breaths. Then, we get the hot towels out and place them on their feet or necks.

Chloe had opened the towel warmer to get her towel out and it was so scalding hot that she screamed in pain and dropped it on the floor. I eyed her in shock.

First of all, to act like that in front of clients was very unprofessional and second, I was confused as to what happened.

We had a maintenance worker look over the towel warmer and he could find nothing wrong with it. He placed a towel in there, warmed it up and it was fine.

Everyone teased Chloe about it after that. She got the nickname "Hot Hands." She seemed to tolerate it decently until something else happened to her and she quit.

Our spa had a sauna adjacent to the changing rooms. If you paid for the deluxe package, customers could get in the sauna or our hot tub before they got dressed and left after their massage.

One of the benefits of working at this Spa was that every night after eight o'clock, any of the masseuses could use the sauna or hot tub free of charge.

Chloe used the sauna on a daily basis. On this particular day, I used it with her. Her last massage ended at eight and I had finished early at seven-thirty.

I beat her to the sauna. I closed my eyes and let the dry heat take me away. I seemed to lose track of time because before long, I could hear the tug of the door and opened my eyes. Chloe waved and took a seat about three feet from me. We were the only employees in there.

I closed my eyes again, enjoying the heat until I heard her scream.

My eyes flew open in shock. I just stared at her. She looked completely pale, shaking and was huddled on the bench in the corner. It was almost as if a giant spider were in the room.

"Chloe, what is going on?"

"Did you see it?" She asked me, her voice wavering.

"See what? No! I had my eyes closed." I scooted towards her and held my hand out in comfort. "Honey, I don't see anything."

"There was a man. He walked in and sat down between us." She gulped. "Then he just faded into nothing."

My pulse started racing and my chest tightened. Had this really happened? Did some creepy apparition just sit next to me and I completely missed it?

I had to admit, I was pretty shaken up by her revelation. I didn't know if it was true or she was just seeing things after a long day at work, but I was never closing my eyes in that sauna again!

Chloe put in her two week notice after that and left the Spa before it was even up. It really bummed me out because when she wasn't freaking out over weird stuff, she was one of the only women there that I got along with.

After Chloe left, I was in charge of hiring a masseuse to replace her. I settled on a guy named Jayden. He had a lot of experience and the spa was really close to his house, so he could walk to work. He even offered to close up at night if we needed it.

One afternoon, Jayden and I were prepping for a couple's massage. He was going to work on the husband and I was going to massage the wife. We led them back to the room, handed them their robes and told them we would be back shortly.

When Jayden and I went back inside the room and whispered we were going to get started, the wife hopped up off of the table, her robe clutched to her chest. "No, no, no" she nervously sputtered, and quickly scurried out of the room.

The husband stared at us in disbelief and followed his wife out of the room. Jayden and I looked at each other in amazement. What had just happened?

I followed the wife to the dressing room and knocked on the stall she was hurriedly dressing in. "Is everything ok? Anything I can do?"

"No, no. I'm leaving."

"Ok." I had paused for a moment, trying to decide what to ask next. "Do you mind telling me what is wrong?"

"You weren't massaging me is what is wrong!" She was almost screaming her words through the closed door.

"I'm sorry. Did we take too long to get back to you?"

"No!" She burst open the stall door and squeezed passed me and out into the lobby.

Pretty much I was dumbfounded. What had just happened? Was this woman mentally disturbed or something?

In the hallway, Jayden came up to me. "Hey," he said. "This is going to sound really weird, but I talked to the husband."

"Ok. Did you find out what the heck is going on?"

"Yeah. So, they heard the door open after we left and thought we came back in.

The wife started feeling someone massaging her shoulders and neck."

"No way."

"Yeah. Then we came in."

I nodded, "So it freaked her the heck out."

"Wouldn't that freak you out?" He chuckled softly and whistled. "Dang. If that really happened, that's some crazy stuff right there. You would tell me if this place was haunted, right?"

That is when I told him about the two incidents that I knew of, and Chloe. Jayden and I both agreed to keep on the lookout for anything "odd" happening in the future and let each other know.

I don't know if you are familiar with a spa, but we play soothing and relaxing music throughout the whole building. It plays on a loop, and the controls for it are up by the checkout desk.

This event was during a massage I was having with a client I see twice a week. Midmassage, the music eerily turned to static. I paused my massage and stared at the speaker in the room waiting for it to resume. It did not right away, so I excused myself and went to investigate.

At the front desk, I found three other masseuses there doing the exact same thing as myself.

"Did you hear it too?" KaCee asked when I approached.

"Yeah. Any idea what is going on with the static?"

"No," she said, her eyes getting wide. "Did you hear IT?"

"What does 'it' mean then?"

"The voice. Ryan heard it, so did Paul," she motioned for them to tell me.

Paul sighed, "I think I heard it."

Annoyed at this point, I asked, "What is 'It?' Come on guys, I'm in the middle of a session. Come out with it already."

Ryan rolled his eyes. 'They think they heard a guy whispering he was going to kill them."

I arched my brow in disbelief. "No, I did not hear that. I heard static."

A few moments later, Jayden said, "Aha! Got it!" And the spa music resumed. We all went our separate ways and finished our sessions.

The next weird event happened to me. If I remember correctly, it was only a few days after the static episode.

After my shift and personal sauna session, I usually go into the dressing room and take a shower.

First, while in the sauna, I swear it sounded like someone sat down on the bench beside me. It creaked like there had been weight put on it. But no one was there but me. I did not see a man like Chloe had described. I just heard the squeaking.

Then, during my shower, I heard the shower next to mine start too. I just assumed it was KaCee.

I turned off my shower and, only a few seconds later, the shower next to me turned off. I grabbed my towel, dried off and wrapped it around me. After I stepped out of the stall, there was no one in the room.

I looked around everywhere. No one. That shower had been going, I swear. I even peered under the stall for feet -- and nothing.

At this point, I really wanted to hurry up, get dressed and get the heck out of there for the day.

When I got to the lockers, every single locker was wide open. They were all closed when I got into the shower.

That was the one incident that really freaked me out. If you were to ask me if the spa is haunted, I'd have to admit that there is definitely something there. What? I'm not sure. Possibly a man because that is what

Chloe saw, but no one else has seen an actual ghost since Chloe left.

There have been whispers in customer's ears while they are getting massages, and a couple of times essential oils have randomly fallen off of the rack by the desk. Other than that, nothing sinister has happened since my shower trauma.

I did try to look up history of the property online, hoping to find some clues as to what may be going on there.

The only thing I could find was a quarter mile away from the Spa. There used to be a mental hospital that burned down in the early 1900's. An electrical fire had killed eight patients. So, if you ask me, I think one of the male patients is messing with us.

I still work there to this day. I have too many repeat clients to think of moving to a different location. I'm just more cautious than I used to be at work. I keep my ears and eyes peeled for unusual things.

CHAPTER SEVEN
Who Screams For Ice Cream?

Sophie and I began working at this ice cream parlor Junior year of high school. It was a fairly easy job and the hours worked perfect with our basketball practice.

It was a classic mom and pop shop. Mr. and Mrs. Teagen were elated to have us there to help. They were nearing retirement age and the shop was becoming too much upkeep for them.

It was decorated like a 70's style ice cream parlor. The counters were a greenish yellow and the flooring was a greenish white floral tile. I honestly thought it needed a modern makeover.

Behind the counter, they had rows and rows of candy. It was kept in these clear plastic containers. They opened from the front for easy scooping. I mean, there had to be around one hundred different candy toppings in those bins. There was no skimping on those!

During our first week of work, when we had just clocked in after practice, Sophie and I began to serve customers. However, every flavor was mixed up.

You see, the flavors were separated into marked bins. But that day not a single flavor was in the correct marked bin. Customers were ordering flavors, and we kept scooping out the wrong ice cream. Frustrated, I told Sophie I would re-organize them while she offered samples to customers.

Once we got everything in the right place and began serving again, the nozzles to the soft serve seemed to turn on their own. Vanilla, chocolate, and swirl ice cream just started pouring out all over the floor.

At this point, we looked at each other, frustrated. This was supposed to be an easy job! But nothing about today had been easy at all. If anything, it had become a complete disaster!

Finally, after closing, we hung up our aprons and were gathering our personal belongings to head out. The lockers were in the back behind the counter.

From the lockers, we heard a loud scraping noise, followed by squeaking and the sound of a million marbles hitting the floor all at once.

Sophie grabbed my hand, white as a sheet.

"Should we call the police?"

I shrugged, shaking, "I don't know."

I mustered enough courage to peer through the curtain that separated the back counter from the locker area. I didn't see anyone. Had we locked the doors? I was pretty sure we locked them.

Sophie gasped and pointed at the floor. Candy was everywhere. Remember how I mentioned the one hundred or so candy toppings? Every bin was open and ALL of them were on the floor. It was an absolute mess!

That evening, after cleaning up the mess, calling the owners and breaking the news, I talked to my mom about it. She dismissed my concerns, explaining that I was being 'too sensitive'. She didn't think anything weird was happening. I guess she figured that teenagers imagine things so, of course, I was just being overly imaginative.

In defeat, I retreated to my bedroom, sat on my bed and called Sophie.

"What just happened tonight?" I'd asked.

"Dude, I don't know but it was creepy!"

"Do you think the Teagens think we did it?"

"Kind of. She was pretty miffed and short with me. What should we do?"

I rolled over on my side to get more comfortable on my bed. And then, through my window in the reflection, it looked like a little girl was standing in my doorway staring at me. She wore a blue dress with white lace around her arms and the bottom of the dress.

I quickly turned towards my doorway and there was not a thing there. No little girl. I jetted back around towards the window and she was no longer in the reflection. Weird.

"Hey, you there?" Sophie was waiting for me to respond.

"Huh- Oh I'm sorry. I thought I saw something."

"What do you mean you thought you saw something?" Sophie's voice expressed worry. "Like what?"

"It's not important. It's been a long day and I must just be tired. See you tomorrow at school?"

"Ya, sounds good. We'll talk then?"

"Ya."

"Ok bye."

I tried not to dwell on the little girl anymore that night. I didn't too much, but I also slept with my light on ...

Sophie and I had to sit down with the Teagens and get a complete lecture. They did not believe our story one bit. They assumed we were fooling around and either purposely or accidentally knocked the candy out. (Which we didn't... obviously.) But we had to sit there like adults and just nod and smile. How fun that was.

We were told that was our one warning and to not let it happen again or we were both getting canned.

We were totally frustrated, but we kept our jobs. The next week went by without anything unusual. I was thankful for that!

Then Saturday happened. It was a busy, crazy day. Being summer, everyone wanted ice cream that weekend.

When closing time came around, we both sighed in relief. Seriously, how many kids could want ice cream in one day? We had served at least a couple hundred kids that day and my feet were aching and sore. All I wanted was to sit down for a second.

"Hey, I'm going to sit for a bit. My feet hurt."

Sophie nodded while sweeping the floor behind the counter. "Ok but don't take too long. My favorite show is coming on in an hour and I don't want to miss it."

I sat down in one of the booths and leaned my head back against the window and just closed my eyes for a minute or two. Is your back supposed to hurt at sixteen? Isn't that an old person thing? Do I need to go to the doctor?

I was pulling out of my thoughts by a sudden, violent shaking. The entire booth was trembling about. Not all of them mind you, just the one I was sitting in.

Sophie stood, broom in hand, mouth agape, just watching me getting tossed around. After a couple seconds, she dropped the broom and helped me out of the booth.

We both stared at each other and then back at the booth. (Which stopped shaking the minute she pulled me out of it, by the way.)

That night, we broke down. We both called the owners and quit. Nope, we didn't put our two week notice in, which could hurt us later on, but we didn't care. We were done with that place.

Sophie and I looked up the address online a few days later when we had a sleepover. I was specifically searching for any reference to or story about a missing little girl. I was convinced that this little girl I saw had to have something to do with what had happened at the parlor.

We found that the ice cream parlor had once been a small grocery store. Two suspects had held up the grocery store and killed the owner and their eight-year-old daughter. Then, they had attempted to set it ablaze.

Emergency responders were able to put out the fire before the entire structure had been damaged. But the building had been torn down to build the ice cream parlor when the Teagen's purchased the land.

CHAPTER EIGHT
Just Toying Around

History has it, the toy store I worked at was built over an old cotton farm. It used to house slaves who would tend to the fields.

One of the slaves was caught sleeping with The Master's daughter. He was not caught in the act but only once she became pregnant.

Story goes, The Master was so infuriated that he tortured the man for days. Lashings galore. Then, once he'd had his fill of cruelty, he shot the man out by a shed. No one knows what became of the child. Had the child been born into a life of labor? Or aborted to avoid family disgrace?

The building in which I worked was new. In fact, it was shiny new. With one glance, you would not even suspect such a terrible thing had happened on the land generations beforehand.

Once you walked into the store, to the left was a small baby section. It housed around fifty or so outfits on hangers, and a few rows of shelving with baby toys. To the right were toys of all ages (mostly toddler and above).

In the back of the store were the video games. About five rows of them. We had two player consoles hooked up to pre-loaded games where children could stop and play while their parents shopped.

It all began during the holiday season. Snow fell outside, families gathered through the doors, trudging their icy footprints everywhere. Check stands were lined with eager Christmas shoppers.

I was working customer service. My job mostly involved scanning items to put on layaway. Suddenly, the intercom buzzed overhead. It almost sounded like a soft static, accompanied by heavy breathing and then a moan.

Reggie was helping me at customer service, and we gave each other a quizzical look.

"Did you do that?" He asked pointing to the intercom.

"No. I was helping her," I motioned at the lady with three rambunctious children running amuck and screaming.

"Weird tacos man, weird tacos." And he was back to helping the gentleman with his bike layaway.

Reggie is an odd guy. He's about thirty, acts like he's sixteen and is obsessed with tacos. Don't ask me why. The guy thinks it's cool to fit tacos into almost anything he does.

Later on that night, Reggie and I were in the back scanning barcodes on bundled layaways and double checking everything was coded and correctly placed before we left.

Jenn, our manager, was the only other person in the store. She was up front counting out registers and locking up.

Reggie put his scanner back. "Ok dude. I'm done. How 'bout you?"

"Almost there. Got one more."

"Ok cool tacos man."

Out of nowhere, there was a crisp and loud "pop pop." It sounded like gunfire. Out of instinct, we both hit the ground, arms shielding our heads. We really thought someone was shooting up the store.

Just then, we heard footsteps closing in on the back room. We were absolutely terrified. We were going to die. I was going to never see my college graduation.

Jenn walked through the doorway, "What the heck are you guys doing?" You could hear the clicking of her nails while she drummed those dagger-like things against the wall in annoyance. "I'd like to leave before morning. Get up and get moving!"

Reggie peered through his arms hesitantly, "Did you hear it?"

Jenn scowled, "Hear what?"

I got to my feet, heart pounding out of my dang chest. "The gunshots."

She scoffed. "You guys are retarded. There were no gun shots. Hurry up and finish your stuff, I'm locking up in five."

For moments, we both were stunned. I've never heard real gunshots before, but if I had, that would definitely be the sound they would make.

We finally brought ourselves back to finishing up, and we did the buddy system in the parking lot. That night was very odd.

Jenn was the opener of the store the next morning. Reggie and I both did not arrive until around eleven. When we arrived, she pulled us both aside.

"You guys trying to pull tricks on me? Listen," a pointed dagger finger at my chest, "we are in holiday season and I don't have time for games." She sent a searing look in Reggie's direction. "You got it?"

We assumed she was referring to the gunshot incident the night beforehand. Later, we came to realize she thought we were taking baby clothing off hangers and throwing them around the store.

We nodded and got back to work.

Nothing else unusual happened until the week of Christmas. It was a mad dash for all the last-minute shoppers. Seriously though, who shops at the last minute during Christmas? Those people are just insane if you ask me.

Remember how I'd mentioned Reggie likes his tacos? Well, he also loves video games. Some nights when Jenn wasn't closing with us, he'd sneak to the game section and play a game or two. At least he DID, until this day.

I should have been working too, but Reggie was really good at games. So, I'd taken a moment out of work as well to watch him play this new game we just got in stock. It was literally his first time playing it and he was kicking butt!

He'd been playing about five minutes and made it a few levels in when the game started glitching. We figured it was just a malfunction in the coding or something. Reggie put the controller away and started to walk away, bummed. Then we heard this low breathing.

For sure it was coming from the game console. We both went over and stuck our ears right up to the speakers on the side. We could hear someone breathing! There is no way in hell that is normal.

Creeped out, we hurried out of there. We did lock up, but we did not finish any of our other duties (which is a whole different story that's boring and involved Jenn yelling).

The last incident happened in the baby section. Jenn was irritated that we skimped on our closing chores so... we got put on baby isle duty for a month!

Reggie had to check the baby clothing and make sure the hanger sizes matched the clothing sizes because clothing mysteriously kept falling off the hangers in the middle of the night.

My duties involved straightening products on the shelves. Bath wash, combs, powder...you name it, I was on it.

Now, I want you to tell me how this is physically possible. Because to me, there is no other explanation for this other than ghosts.

I was working on lining up the baby powder on the shelves. Jenn was being a jerk and insisted the powder be in exact straight lines, not one container could be off by a millimeter. (Her exact words – she's kind of strict when she's miffed).

I looked down to grab a few other containers and when I looked up, one of the baby powders fell over front ways, so the top was directly in front of my face. I'm going to stop here and remind you that these containers have a safety seal on them. But somehow this particular item did not.

Just as I reached up to stand it back upright, I watched a phantom hand squeeze the container and powder littered my face. Now you tell me how that happens when there is a safety seal on them? And what made the container indent like a hand was squeezing it?

My vision was blurred. Erratically, I wiped at my eyes to clear the powder from my vision. As I did so, I heard one word whispered in my ear that seemed to trail off, "B-a-b-yyyyyy-"

Yup. That about did it for me. I ran out of the isle, tripping along the way because powder was still all over my face and shirt. I looked at Reggie horrified, and Reggie looked at me like I was a crazy taco.

Jenn saw the commotion and hustled over. "What are you doing? Playing with the baby products? Urgh. I can't leave you alone for one minute!"

With all my might, I held back from screaming in her face. How could she work here and not notice the weird things happening! I ripped off my badge and handed it to her. I was done. I wanted out of that place.

Since that day, I have never been back. Not even for a gift. I buy my gifts for my nieces and nephews elsewhere.

And, in case you are curious, Reggie and I kept in touch. He still works there, and he still loves his tacos.

CHAPTER NINE
Readers Beware

Literature interested me the most in life. Is there truly anything that smells better than the pages of a brand-new book? I lived for that smell. That smell drove me into a career I would begin to fear.

As long as I can remember, I was a literary nerd. My parents would tease me because I would open a book, any book, and just devour it in a matter of hours. Fiction was my favorite.

I loved being able to picture myself in these amazing worlds that others had created. I truly was a dreamer. Maybe that's why no one seemed to believe me at first. But once they came to the bookstore and it happened in front of them, they were believers too.

It was a day in December. I remember because we had just had our first snowfall and I was thoroughly excited to wear my brand-new jacket. I saved two months to buy that gaudy thing.

I trudged up the stairs, arms full to the brim with books. I was excited to check these books back in and check out many more. This was something of a perk of my job. No library fees... ever!

I placed the books on the counter, grabbed the scanner and started checking them back into the computer. That's when I heard the first noise. It was a flappy noise. As if pages were flapping. Then, a thud.

Confused and slightly concerned, I rose from my chair and went to investigate. I was the only person there yet. I had not unlocked the doors behind me when I had arrived.

First, I went into the mystery section, which is where I thought the noise had come from. Nothing unusual there. Then, I explored the horror section. Something peculiar. A row of books were off the shelves. Not just on the floor randomly mind you, laying perfectly on their backs as if someone had laid them there. All were open to exactly page thirty-five. Huh.

I shook off the creepiness of the encounter and easily placed them back on the shelf where they belonged.

Back at the counter, I was stamping the books with their check-in dates and double checking that they had entered correctly into the computer. Everything seemed to match, so I started the journey of putting them back to 'their homes' as I call it.

Romance fiction is one of my favorites, so most of them ended up there. What single female doesn't love her romantic fiction, am I right?

I had nearly all put back in their homes, except two. From behind me I heard the creaking of floorboards. I furrowed my brow in confusion and listened for a moment. There it was again!

I peered over my shoulder, to see no one. (As expected, because as I said before, I was the only one there.) I then resumed finding the places for the other two books I'd checked out.

After I had placed the last one, I could have sworn I felt something against my cheek. It is hard to explain, but I will try. It felt like a cold wind with very delicate wisps. Almost like a cloud, but that cloud had just momentarily brushed against my cheek.

The experience sent a chill through me, and the hairs on the back of my neck were surely at attention. I tried my best to shake off the experience and get back to the desk. I strolled to grab my keys.

A few expected regulars followed me as I unlocked the door. "Good morning May, good morning Albert," I smiled. "What is on the menu today?"

"Oh, you know me," May chirped, "Anything that's spicy!"

We both giggled, and I gave her shoulder a squeeze. "I'll be right behind the desk if you need me, hun."

"Sounds wonderful, thank you."

Albert was an absolute sweetheart. He was pudgy and balding, but beyond his looks for his middle-age, the man was a true gem. He always had a cute little joke for me. I think it was one of the things I looked forward to most when I opened the library.

The man was like clockwork. He was retired at forty-eight, and the library was his first stop after breakfast. Sometimes, he'd even bring me a coffee from the diner if it was too chilly outside.

By the way, I must add here that yes, Albert was flirting with me. And we are happily married now.

As I sat at the desk, Albert eyed me, "You ready for today's joke?"

"Am I ever! Lay it on me sir!"

"Alright. Here she goes," He appeared momentarily deep in thought, "Why is a young lady like an arrow?"

"Why?" I shrugged, my eyes wide awaiting the punchline.

His adorable pudgy frame jiggled as he chuckled, "Because they are all aquiver in the presence of a beau."

"Oh Albert," I rose from my seat and came around to embrace him, "you always know how to make me laugh."

"You know it!"

"What is the literary find for today," I questioned.

"Oh, you know me, I love the war books."

"Do you need any help finding one? I can see if I can find something intriguing in my computer."

"Thanks, but no. Browsing around is the best part!"

At that moment, both of us were in a bubble. Nothing else seemed to exist. We were one with each other's silly smiles and gazes. At least until we heard May scream. Not just any scream. The bloody murder, someone just died kind of scream.

In horror, we both went running. Sprinting towards the romantic fiction section. (I made it there a little faster than Albert…)

"It burns! It burns!" May was screaming and running her hands up and down the sleeves of her jacket.

"What burns?" We asked in unison.

"I don't know!" She cried.

I hastily tugged at her jacket and tossed it on the floor. May pulled up her sleeves and revealed three scratches on each arm.

"Something scratched me! I saw this mist float from over there," she pointed to the end of isle, "to right here and disappear in the books. That's when I felt this incredible pain."

Albert looked at me, and I shrugged. I didn't know what on earth to think of this. In my life, I've never seen or heard of anything like this before. As the millennials say these days, 'My mind was blown.'

Luckily, these occurrences were the only that I can recount to you besides a few minor floor creaks, and phantom footsteps.

However, a few teenagers swore up and down that they heard footsteps, and no one was visible.

CHAPTER TEN
You Live You Learn

I had begun my fifth year of teaching. I normally taught first graders, but this year was my first year teaching sixth graders.

New year, new school, new me. I had one heck of a teaching job fall in my lap. My neighbor, Joe, was actually the principal at the middle school I moved to. He made me a slightly better offer than I was getting.

Joe did mention to me that the position in this classroom opened up quite often. Frustrated, he had turned to me since we were friends. I kindly accepted the job with the small pay increase. On a teacher's salary, every little bit helps!

On the first day of school, I introduced the class to the class pet. I had bought them a Winter White hamster which I named Gigi. She was sweet and cute!

All the kids arose from their seats to have a look at her. Some of the girls swooned. "She's such a cutie!" "Omg I love her!" "Can I take her home?"

After about fifteen minutes, I seated everyone to get started. I had a power point made of this year's curriculum I wanted to show them.

A minute or two into the presentation, the projector just shut off. I walked over and unplugged everything, before plugging it back in. It came to life again. Weird. Maybe it was faulty?

Throughout the presentation, three or four more times the projector glitched. It would turn off. I'd jingle the cords or unplug and replug and it was raring to go.

A presentation that should have been only five minutes long had turned into nearly forty-five. Not that uncommon right? First days of school are always about working the kinks out.

After the power point, I had the kids break into groups to get to know each other better. During this time, a smell lingered and went away, then came back.

I went over to open the window to get some fresh air in the classroom. The smell could best be described as, rotting pickles? It was not the most pleasant smell.

All the while, I had to keep reeling the kids back in. They started making fart jokes. Then they found a kid they didn't care for very much, and he became the culprit for the smell (although he wasn't).

About a half hour before the end of the day, two things happened. First, I had the kids doing quiet time. They could read or draw, but it had to be quiet. And it was, except a random cough here or there or someone clearing their throat.

Suddenly, a chair squeaked. I know what you are thinking, and it wasn't like that at all. It was a squeak chairs made when being sat on. There was only one empty chair in the entire class.

The noise raised everyone's attention to the empty chair in the center of the third row of seats. Some kids looked horrified, while others looked amused. I tried my best to look calm, like it didn't affect me what-so-ever.

"Ignore it." I instructed. "Back to quiet time." The kids turned their attention back to what they were doing.

A few moments later, the chair again squeaked. Everyone's heads were up and looking at the empty seat. To all our bewilderment, it ever so slightly moved to the right. Just a hair, but enough to notice.

So that was that. I ended quiet time. I turned the class focus to the board and began to write a small homework assignment on it. That's when it hit me. A book hit me square in the back of the head.

I turned around, expecting laughing and chuckling. Instead, I was greeted with faces of absolute horror. I was so confused. I did not know how to handle any of this. Was someone trying to prank me?

I kept my composure for the last twenty minutes of school. I sighed relief when the bell rang and students filed out eagerly.

Joe came in to check on me before leaving for the day.

"How was the first day?" He asked.

I blew out of a gush of air, "Well, you could say it was a day."

"That bad huh?"

"I think one of the kids is pranking me."

"Oh? Which one?"

"No idea." I shuffled the papers on my desk looking for tomorrow's agenda. I was trying to finish it up so I could leave and go home.

"Well if you figure it out, send them to my office. I have a zero-tolerance policy."

I looked at him favorably, "I appreciate that Joe. Thank you."

With a wave, he was gone, and I was left to finish tomorrow's planning.

A loud bang from behind startled me. It sounded like someone had thrown a chair into the wall. I quickly got up to check the classroom next door.

Confusion washed over me. The classroom was dark, and the door was locked. No one was in there. Well that was odd.

I shrugged and went back into my room. At that point I was just thinking that I needed to pack up so I could leave.

I was over at my desk, bent over, shoving some folders and papers into my bag that I wanted to take with me and work on more at home. Then, I heard the door latch click and the door creak open.

What the heck was going on today! I was still bent over, peering over my shoulder at the door. It was now obviously open and I could hear footsteps on the linoleum floor.

They were coming towards my direction... but no one was there!

I kept blinking my eyes, as if I blinked them enough, the door would actually be shut, and this would all be my imagination. But no. The door was still open, and footsteps were stopping right in front of me.

I was terrified. Frozen in place. I was looking straight ahead at nothing, but thinking it has to be something.

And just like that, the footsteps started receding, like they were headed back out the door. Then the door started to shut and the latch clicked. What the heck just happened?

I grabbed my bag, half full of what I wanted, and ran out of the classroom to my car. I was done with that room. I could not be there a minute longer.

The next day, I truly contemplated quitting. But then I thought I was being silly. Maybe the grade change and the school change were stressing me out more than I thought. So, I chose to stick it out.

After lunch, we were working on Geography. The kids had their books open and were studying it quietly.

Overhead the fire alarm sounded. The kids perked their heads up, hopped out of their seats and lined up at the door.

I was not worried how to handle this. I'd studied the handbook and emergency charts the school had given me. I had this down. But usually, when they are planning a drill, they notify the teachers. I wasn't notified.

I led the kids outside to the spot allotted for our class, but no one else was out there. It was eerie. I wondered if maybe they were slower than us? Then, when another minute passed, I held the sheet up to my face and studied it. Maybe I had the wrong spot. Could it have been on the other side of the building? So, I led the kids to the other side. No one.

The kids began laughing and conversing between themselves while I stood there dumbfounded.

Joe appeared from a side door. "Hey Coleen, everything ok?"

"Where is everyone?"

He arched a brow, "What do you mean?"

"The fire drill. How come we are the only class to come out?"

He looked at me like I was absolutely nuts. "There is no... fire drill."

So, I took that moment to be proactive. I told Joe that I quit. No two weeks notice, no nothing. And I went back to teaching first graders.

After asking other staff at that school about these occurrences, I found out that, a few months before the previous school year ended, a boy in that classroom had a seizure and died. He was the kind of kid who was always picking on others and clowning around when he shouldn't be.

I was the third teacher to quit. The other two quit after their first day. Most of the staff was amazed I showed up for the second day.

CHAPTER ELEVEN
Haunted Kennel

I loved my job. I had always wanted to work with animals, but my mother was struggling with MS and I did not feel like leaving her side to go away to college to get a veterinarian degree. As a compromise to myself, I took a job at a local kennel.

For the most part, the kennel wasn't that spooky, so I actually still work there. However, there were a few things I witnessed in the four years I have been there.

One of the first was during a week where the kennel was mostly dead. We only had two dogs boarded, which meant the rest of the place was getting a deep cleaning. (It's much easier to deep clean when there's hardly any animals present.)

I went into a room that had 10 kennels. It was completely empty, not a single dog in the room. As I was spraying the concrete down and collecting blankets and putting them in a pile to be washed, I saw one of the blankets move towards one of the kennels as if a dog was tugging it back inside to keep warm.

It was odd, but I convinced myself I had manufactured the whole thing and went about my business.

After I had collected the blankets and washed the concrete, I took the blankets to the laundry. I went back to the room to wind up the hose and turn off the lights.

On the wet concrete floor were paw prints. They went from one side of the kennel to the other as if a dog was pacing down the rows. There was no way for a dog to be in that room. However, I double checked each kennel to make sure. There was no dog.

For that, I had zero explanation. I was completely stumped and a little freaked out to be honest.

Later that afternoon, Joey and I went back into that same kennel to grab some supplies from the supply closet. (I did not want to go back in there by myself, so I made him go with me.)

First of all, when we opened the door there was an overwhelmingly strong odor of wet dog. But I had just cleaned the kennel and it hadn't smelled when I was done.

Second, if you listened closely, which we did, you could hear a dog whining. Joey went through each of the kennels, as I had earlier, and found nothing.

We couldn't explain it. We had both heard it. Joey was slightly shaken, I believe, but trying to put on a brave face.

Then, we went and got supplies from the supply closet. As Joey was loading my arms full of some blankets and bedding, we heard a scratching noise.

I sat the blankets down and we nodded at each other to investigate. We walked as slightly as we could on the concrete, listening.

When we got to the third kennel, you could hear that the sound was its loudest there. We exchanged glances and opened the kennel door. There was nothing inside. Not a thing to make a sound like that. Then, we heard the whining again. That, however, was barely audible. But you *could* hear it.

We had previously housed the sweetest little Doberman for a couple who were going on their honeymoon. His name was Bacon. Bacon was such a sweetie. But he was old, tired and had terminal cancer.

The couple hadn't wanted to board him, but they didn't know what else to do so they could go on their honeymoon. The second day we had had him, he had complications and passed away.

Joey and some of the others think Bacon is still there, roaming the kennels sometimes. Myself on the other hand, I'm not sure what I believe. But some things you just can't explain.

CHAPTER TWELVE
Maybe It's Broken

This story is about a car wash I worked at one summer while saving for college. At first, I thought the owner just needed to upgrade some of the equipment which was faulty.

Sometimes, the sprayers would spray soap instead of water, or vice versa. I blamed this on a guy I worked with. I thought maybe he was loading the wrong stuff into the wrong sprayers.

One day, I went with him and watched him load everything. I was getting miffed that people were complaining. He did everything correct.

I went back and helped some cars pay and watched as they went through. The sprayers sprayed the wrong stuff again. I had no explanation for that, so I told the owner to think about buying new ones.

Then cars would just stop in the middle of a wash and not move anymore. We had to look at the electrical and it was fine. No explanation for that either.

Then, one day, I was getting my own car washed. I was to the part of the wash where the soap was going (working correctly on this day) and the windows were all soaped up.

As clear as day, a handprint appeared on my front windshield in front of my face. I knew no one had climbed on my car. I would have felt it or heard something.

Still to this day, I have no explanation for any of this. The owner had the equipment looked at. The soap and water were fine, the track is fine, no faulty wiring.

CHAPTER THIRTEEN
Lease Breaker

My boyfriend and I had just broken up, so I had moved out and into a one-bedroom apartment with my cat Trixie.

It was a little rough for the wear, but it was all I could find in my price range with such last-minute noticc.

At first, I noticed the cat would sit in the kitchen tussling its tail around and just staring at the corner. Sometimes it would hiss and arch its back, but most of the time it would just sit there, intrigued.

Mostly, I tried to ignore it. However, one morning I was making a pot of coffee. I was late for work and trying to brush my hair while I waited for the coffee to brew.

All of the sudden, it was like ice brushing my shoulder. I felt cold tingles down my arm, standing my hair on end. I shivered. I walked over and checked the thermostat and it was set at the usual temperature, so I shrugged it off as my imagination.

When I got home from work that day, I was greeted by Trixie. She was running in between my legs, purring and meowing for her dinner. I set my purse on the counter, got her food out of the pantry and filled her bowl.

Half-way through eating she just stopped. She sat down and just stared. Nothing came between Trixie and her food. This was really weird! That is when I started paying closer attention.

I was boiling some pasta on the stove for my easy bachelorette dinner. Trixie was sleeping on the couch, sprawled in every direction (because she's just a couch hog like that).

While I was stirring the pasta and humming to myself, from behind me I heard something slide off of the counter and contents spill on the floor. I whipped around and found my purse on the floor. Makeup, keys and money were littered on the tile.

I stood there arching my brow trying to figure out how that happened. It wasn't even close to the edge. I peered around the door frame and Trixie was awake now and alert, but still on the couch. Weird.

I crouched down and started picking up items and stuffing them back in my purse. That's when the air got really heavy and dense. It's hard to explain.

An audible whisper said, "Goooooo."

I dropped my purse on the floor and ran into the living room and called my sister. I asked her to come over because I was freaked out. Luckily, she only lived two blocks away and came right over.

Hannah and I sat on the couch and watched a movie to get my mind off of things after I finished my pasta. She asked if I wanted her to spend the night, but I said no. The more I thought about what happened, the more I felt silly and maybe that I had just imagined it after a long day at work and too much stress in my life.

Around ten o'clock, she headed out and I went to take a shower. I was in there trying to not think about anything that happened that day at home, as well as keep my mind from veering in that direction. Then I heard a weird, squeaky noise.

My hair was lathered up and I was worried that if I opened my eyes, I was going to get soap in them. I was shaking because it happened when I couldn't possibly see, so I washed as much soap as I could out of hair and off of my face so I could open an eye.

On the glass door was a distinct handprint. But because I wasn't able to look at it right away, it was already starting to fog over and fade away. The freakiest thing about that handprint was, if you are in the shower, the fog is on the inside of the door not the outside. So, whatever made the hand print was in there with me.

I didn't even rinse the last bit of shampoo out of my hair. I turned the water off, threw the shower door open and ran out of there as fast as I could, no towel and all.

I ran to my bedroom, grabbed my cell phone and immediately dialed Hannah. I begged her to come back and spend the night with me.

We talked about my options. I had just signed a lease and there was no way to get out of it. Hannah offered for me to move in with her for a couple of months so I could break the lease and move out.

I had that entire apartment packed in two days. I did not spend another night there either. That night, I grabbed what clothes I needed and stayed at her house. And when it came time to move my stuff out, I had other people there with me.

CHAPTER FOURTEEN
Upstairs On The Left

My wife and I were celebrating five years of married bliss. After quite a few discussions about how to celebrate and treat ourselves, we settled on a cozy Bed and Breakfast two towns over.

The day we checked in was the day I should have turned the car around. I should have said, "You know honey, the mountain spa sounds way better." But... I didn't.

The building was older, which originally was why it charmed us in the first place. But, as we walked through the front doors, you could feel it.

The air was heavy, and the place just had a terribly bad energy about it. I shrugged it off as being in an unfamiliar place and chose not to mention it to my wife.

We checked in to our room and headed up the stairs to the first door on the left. My wife's face was beaming. She had always wanted to try a Bed and Breakfast. I smirked to myself over her joy.

Once in our room, suitcases on top of the bed, my wife turned to me, "So this is going to sound a little crazy."

My eyebrow arched and my interest was peeked, "Ok."

"Did you get a weird feeling downstairs like you were being watched?"

I contemplated on how to respond. I definitely felt something odd, but I had not felt like I was being watched.

"We just had a long drive, maybe your mind was just wandering a bit. Why don't I run you a bath?"

I could see that my answer frustrated her, but I didn't believe in ghosts.

Silent defeat fell over her face and she nodded.   "Yes, maybe that will help."

After her bath, we had dinner at a nearby restaurant. It had come highly recommended by the owner, and I have to say I was pleasantly surprised. The food was very good.

"Do you mind if we go for a walk and see the town?" My wife asked after dinner.

"No, that sounds great!"

We walked about three blocks, taking photos along the way. Then we walked back to the Bed and Breakfast and we took some photos out in front as well.

"We should probably get ourselves to bed," I reminded, "we have a few things planned around seven tomorrow."

"Oh yes, I almost forgot!"

While we made our way to our room, this time I did not notice a heavy feeling. Everything seemed as it should be. I must have been tired from the drive as well, who knows.

At 2:45 am, I awoke to the covers being ripped off of me and something attempting to jerk me off of the bed by my ankle.

I could make out a black shadowy figure, and that was all. Terrified, thinking someone broke into our room, I quickly shook myself free and turned the light on, only to see the shadow instantly disappear. Nothing was in our room. All the while, my wife was sleeping soundly next to me, only half of the covers on her. I swear she could sleep through an earthquake!

I did not go back to sleep that night. I turned the light back off and sat on the sofa, watching tv. Every little noise perked my ears.

By seven o'clock, I was delirious. I made an excuse to my wife as if I was coming down with a stomach bug. I asked if we could cancel and do the activities later in the day. I could tell she was bummed, but she agreed.

Finally, I got some rest. Nothing tried jerking me off of the bed, and the air was as it should be. I slept for about three hours or so.

Just as I was waking up, my wife put the digital camera in my face. "Hey--- what are you doing?" I snipped.

"Just look." Her face was all concern.

I sighed. I had only been awake about a minute. I hastily grabbed the camera from her and started flipping through the photos.

"Specifically, the ones out front of the Bed and Breakfast," she directed.

I shot her a look of annoyance and flipped faster through the photos. When I got to the pictures she was referring to, my blood ran cold. I blinked my eyes to make sure I was viewing this correctly.

"So, what exactly do you think you saw in these?" I asked, lifting my head to face her.

"Exactly what you think you are seeing right now."

I turned my attention back to the camera, amazed and terrified at the same time. I did not believe in ghosts, but this place was haunted.

The figure I had seen in our room trying to pull me off of the bed? He was in every one of our photos. The photos in front of the Bed and Breakfast were the creepiest.

In the others, he was far away. Barely seen in the shots. But the closer we walked and snapped, the closer he was in every shot. Then, when we photographed the Bed and Breakfast, he was literally so close behind us that we should have felt his breath on our necks.

The last photo looked as if his distorted hand was around my wife's throat. He didn't have a face. He was all black. A black shadow. But you could tell by how his black shadow hand wisped over the front of her neck that he was sinister.

Needless to say, we did not finish our stay there. One and done. And we do not go to Bed and Breakfast's for any reason. It was an anniversary neither of us will forget.

CHAPTER FIFTEEN
Starving Artist

I was a painter. Always creating. Alone in my own world of dreams and thoughts. I could paint for hours. On one occasion, I painted for a day and a half straight. I was on a roll and I didn't want to stop until it was finished. It was going to be my best work yet.

We had lived in the house for about two years. Nothing out of the ordinary had ever happened before. At least, not that I had noticed.

I was eighteen and I had taken a year off before committing to college. I wanted to explore my painting. I wanted to be seen. I had to get my work out there. This was a career I'd wanted to pursue since I was able to walk.

Now, I'm not one of those sucky creative types. I didn't have an unrealistic dream what-so-ever. I was good. Damn good. I had sold paintings to parents of my friends for years. But I wanted more. I wanted the whole world to see what I could do. I wanted my name known on other continents.

One night, while online doing some hunting for new fresh ideas, I saw a photo during my search that intrigued me. I clicked on it. An article popped up that seemed to have been written just for me.

It was a spell you could do with a black candle in front of a mirror in the dark. You needed to prick your finger once, allow a drop of blood to fall onto the wick and then light the candle.

According to the article, you then stared deep into the mirror for however many minutes you could muster, repeating out loud what you wanted. Before you asked for what you desired, you were to say, "Mistress of Evil, Mistress of Greed, these are the things I hope to succeed."

Call me crazy, but the whole idea peaked my interests. I went to a local wiccan shop and bought a black candle and a lighter.

Did I think some magic words and a candle were going to create my destiny for me? Not really, but it couldn't hurt trying, right? Or could it?

So, that evening once my parents had gone to bed, I sat my easel next to my bedroom mirror. I figured it would help me stay focused on what I wanted; keep the image of my dream fresh in my mind as I did the mini ritual.

I turned off all of the lights and felt my way back to the mirror. I fumbled on the counter for the candle then picked it up. I used a safety pin to prick my finger and took a deep breath. Here goes nothing.

A droplet of blood landed on the wick and I slowly rose the lighter and lit the candle.

In the darkness, I could hear myself breathe. Slow, cautious breaths. I looked deep into my mirror. Concentrated. Hoping. I want to be famous. Help me be famous. Painting is my entire being.

I began to whisper at the mirror, "Mistress of Evil, Mistress of Greed, these are the things I hope to succeed."

I paused, listening. Nothing was happening.

"I want to be a famous painter. I want people other than friends and family to buy my paintings. Mistress of Evil, Mistress of Greed, these are the things I hope to succeed."

Nothing spooky happened. I actually thought it was all a stupid hoax. I blew out the candle and turned my bedside lamp on and read for a while before falling into a deep sleep.

It was an unnerving dream. A horrible dream. It is a dream I am sure I will remember forever.

In my dream, I was walking up an old rotted staircase. Along the wall, paintings were hung. They appeared old and tattered. The family faces that were painted appeared to be rotting, but not from age or wear.

A certain painting stood out to me the most. It was of a young girl. Her skin was white, her eyes black holes. She leaned on her hands in a serene pose. Her nails were impressively long. Her hair was a brownish chocolate that seemed to flow to her mid-back. Upon her face were gashes. It was painted that way.

How odd, I thought in my dream. But I kept climbing the stairs, seeing morbid painting after morbid painting. In one, there was a man, in tattered clothing, standing next to a shovel with a sinister smirk on his face. He too had pale white skin and black holes for eyes.

In the background of the painting was a barn that looked like our barn. And a freshly dug grave with a cross directly behind him.

I finally reached the top of the stairs, the wallpaper peeling off of the walls. The floorboards creaked slightly under my feet and in the distance could hear the steady drip of a leaky faucet.

Every step I took, the dripping got faster and closer.

Drip….drip….drip.

Drip…Drip…Drip.

Drip..Drip..Drip.

A door on my left was ajar and echoed the sounds. It had to be coming from there. I walked inside. It was a bathroom.

As soon as I walked in, I realized I was now in my own bathroom. In my own house.

I turned my bathroom light on and looked around. It was my sink, my toothbrush on the counter, my mirror. Weird.

In a few moments, I had studied the whole room. Everything was in its place as in my own bathroom. And the noises continued.

The dripping appeared to come from the bathtub, where the curtain was drawn. This is probably the point where everyone yells at the television, "Don't open it! Get out of there!"

And possibly in my unconscious mind, I was thinking similar thoughts. But, I figured it was a dream and I could wake myself up.

As I reached out to open the curtain, the dripping stopped. I stood there with my arm outstretched, unsure if I should open the curtain at all now.

Losing my courage to open the curtain, I turned to rush out of the bathroom. The man from the painting face to face with me, shovel in hand.

He did not scream at me, nor try to impale me with the shovel. He just stared at me with his eyeless sockets.

I awoke from my dream, drenched in sweat. It wasn't the scariest dream I had ever had, but surely the oddest.

For the rest of the night, I decided to stay up and just paint while watching some television to get my mind off of things.

Around six in the morning, my eyes were heavy and I started dosing in and out in front of my easel. I put the caps back on all my paints, put my brushes in the sink and tucked myself back into bed.

This time I did not dream. It was a peaceful sleep.

I awoke around noon or so. I stretched and yawned. I looked around my room, remembering the nightmare from earlier. Sunlight was beaming in and birds were chirping outside my window.

I got out of bed and walked over to my dresser to brush my hair. As I was brushing, I gazed over at my easel to see how well my middle of the night painting turned out. I dropped the brush.

My mouth dropped open wide and I just couldn't stop staring at the painting.

I had painted the man and child from my dream. They were standing in front of the barn. The little girl smiled, eyeless, holding my decapitated head in one hand and a saw in the other. The man sneered at his daughter, my lifeless body at his feet.

I tried to find the website again that had the ritual and the photo. I searched online for two days and could not find it anywhere. Did I release some sort of demon from this ritual? Or am I just having crazy dreams that, when I'm tired, I paint without remembering?

I will say, my friend Anna saw the painting and was shocked. I usually painted happier things. She told me she was worried about me being depressed to have painted something so morbid. She advised me to throw the painting out.

I did just that too. I walked with her out to our trash bins and she watched me throw it in there and close the lid.

An hour or so later, there was a knock at the door. Anna was still there with me.

I answered the door and it was a man I did not know. He looked about twenty-five, had a goth look, complete with septum and bridge piercings.

"Can I help you?" I'd asked.

"Yes. Your painting is getting wet." He held up the painting I had thrown in the trash.

Anna and I looked at each other. "Did you go through my trash?" I was pissed.

"No. It was sitting by your front door and I noticed it while I was walking by."

"You can buy it if you want," Anna chimed in.

I was not sure how much I believed him, honestly. However, I was curious how much he was willing to pay. So, I quoted him two hundred dollars.

He agreed and bought it. He pulled out a wallet with a chain attached and handed me four fifty-dollar bills, thanked me and walked off.

Again, Anna and I exchanged glances and shut the door.

DARKNESS WINS

Sneak Peak

Headlights

Carrie and her daughter Lily were just finishing moving their stuff into their new home. It was a beautiful two-story house with three bedrooms on a three-acre lot.

Post divorce, Carrie had been stressed. The drain of finding the new place to call home, as well as the pressure of finding something in the same school district that was affordable had taken a toll on her. At night, she was always exhausted, but her mind would just not shut off.

Two days after moving in, boxes still litered the house everywhere. Carrie had broken down and finally decided to go into the doctor. He prescribed her a sleeping aide, which she hoped would help give her the energy needed to finish unpacking.

Returning from the pharmacy, she made herself a cup of tea and decided to sit out on her lovely new porch. The porch wrapped around the front of her home like a welcoming hug. Chesnut wood planks, a porch swing, and a handcrafted bench all made the scene inviting. The porch also overlooked the huge front yard, which was bordered with trees.

The warm steam from her cup danced up and away from its brim, and she wondered if there was anything better than this house. For her price range and the land it held, this house had been quite the steal. Why would anyone let this beautiful property go for so cheap?

She noticed a tall man with a grey beard walking down her drive. He wore overalls that looked quite raggy for the wear. He sauntered with light brisk steps, eyes to the dirt drive. She was pretty sure he had not even noticed her sitting on the porch.

As he was in ear shot from the porch, she stood. "Hello there," she called to him.

His bearded face lifted and he half-smiled, "Hello."

"Can I help you?"

"Oh, not really," He pulled a tobacco pipe from his overall pocket, lit it with care and took a drag. "Name is Doug Chesterfelt. Was just welcoming you. I'm your closest neighbor. 'Bout 3 miles that way," he pointed down the street.

"Long way for a welcome walk," she smiled, as her eyes squinted against the afternoon sun.

"Doctor's orders. Have to walk at least three miles a day," he chuckled. "I figure today if I double that, it will make him extra happy."

She lifted her tea and took the last sip, nodding in reply.

"Well, don't be a stranger. The Mrs. and I are just down the road if you need us. Her name is Susan." He turned around and waved over his shoulder, "I best be getting on my way back, these old legs are slower than they used to be."

"Thanks for stopping by!" She called.

The evening was winding down and Carrie and her daughter were perched on their couch, watching the last five minutes of a scary movie and buried deep in blankets.

A flash from the window made them both jump almost out of their skin. They turned to each other with quizzical looks on their faces.

"Mom? What is that?" Lily's voice was timid and shaking.

"I'm not sure honey, I will go look, ok?" Carrie got to her feet and hesitantly approached the window. Once she recessed the blinds, the whole room was flooded with highbeams.

"What the-?"

"Mom, what is that?" Lily cried out.

Carrie waved a hand to shush her daughter as she tried to squint through the glare and understand what was causing it.

"It looks...like..." she peered her face up the glass and cupped her hands around her face, "A car or something? With it's brights on?"

"But why would they be in our driveway, it's so far off of the road?" Lily was now hunched behind the couch.

"I have no idea." Carrie picked up her cell phone and dialed 911. She explained the situation and officers were notified. She was told to check all her doors and windows and was promised they would be there soon.

As quietly as possible she went through her house room by room, with Lily on her heels, checking every window, and door. They were all locked tight. She glanced at the clock, 12:20am.

Once satisfied everything was secure, Carrie ushered Lily into the kitchen and away from the madening light, hoping to regain some sanity until the officers came. It was the most awkward of silences. They both sat at the kitchen table, mute, shaking and constantly darting their eyes around at the shadows.

Carrie dared not turned on the kitchen light so as to not draw unwanted attention to their current location in the house. She had never had anything this freaky happen to her before.

From outside there was a low rumble, and the cascading lights finally disappeared. Lily and Carrie looked at each other in the now utter darkness. Were they gone?

At that exact moment, a pounding on the front door sent them both jumping out of their chairs and into each others' arms.

"Police! Everything alright?"

Nothing was alright about this night at all. Carrie made her way to the front door and told the officers what had occurred. It was a sleepless night.

Most of the boxes had finally been unpacked. Lily was an angel and had really stepped in and helped out. Carrie was finally feeling like the house was liveable now except... for the night before.

As to be expected, she mulled over the events multiple times throughout the day. Had they both been so tired that they had freaked out over nothing?

The police said the light could have been from the highway. Perhaps someone had stopped briefly on the side of the road, or someone had hit something and pulled over long enough to move it off into the bushes.

None of these explainations felt quite right, however. But she had made a police report and was finally feeling slightly resolved.

"Mom!"

"Yes?" Carrie called from the kitchen, finishing the last of the dinner dishes.

"I'm setting up Monopoly, will you play with me?"

She quickly glance at the clock, "Sure honey, give me five more minutes to get these loaded and I will be in there."

"Ok, mom."

Monopoly was one of Lily's favorite games and boy was she good at it! More often then not, she won and it wasn't even close. The girl had mad negotiating skills. And for this particular Saturday night, it was like any other. She had almost used every hotel in the box, and all but three of the houses.

"Can't we just say you won?" Carrie yawned. Neither had gotten much sleep after last night's light debacle.

"Awe... but you still have one house left you can mortgage before I win." Lily frowned but nodded. "I guess it is getting late." Both girls peered at the clock. It was fifteen after midnight.

Carrie began putting the pieces and the money back in the box. "Hey, can you help me take the trash out after we get this put away?"

Lily smirked, "What do I get in return?"

"A roof over your head."

"Awe, you're no fun mom."

They both chuckled and headed for the kitchen.

Outside was slightly brisk, around fifty degrees. Summer was sure turning into fall at a steady pace. Carrie carried the kitchen trash and Lily held a few broken down boxes from unpacking.

When they neared the trash cans, it was there again, an overwhelming light. That blinding, seething light! They both dropped their trash and ran back towards the house.

"Mom, I think it's happening again," said Carrie shakily, reaching for her cell phone to call the police.

"Me too sweety, me too."

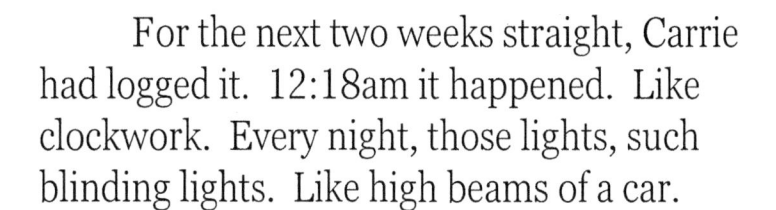

For the next two weeks straight, Carrie had logged it. 12:18am it happened. Like clockwork. Every night, those lights, such blinding lights. Like high beams of a car.

They shined in no other room than the living room, and usually no longer than a minute or two.

She was sure the police were starting to think she was a nut job. By the time they arrived each time, the lights were gone and there was no evidence of anything. She was starting to think she was imagining it too. But if she was, how could Lily be seeing the same exact thing?

She woke to a sunny day. It seemed like it should be a bright and cheery day, but considering their home life in the new house, most days were just not cheerful.

Carrie held her shopping list in one hand, and a basket in the other. They were already out of milk and bread and numerous other things.

Suddenly, she was bumped from behind while reaching for a loaf of bread off of the shelf. Carrie jumped into the air like a cat after seeing a cucumber.

"Oh dear, I'm so sorry." The woman held out a wrinkly hand in apology. "I'm Susan. I'm not as good on my feet these days I'm afraid. Always bumping into this and that."

"No worries," Carrie offered, while silently taking calming breaths, "I'm Carrie Carter."

"Oh! You are the gal who is my neighbor. How lovely to meet you." A warm smiled lined her face.

"Susan Chesterfelt?"

"In the flesh my dear."

"I met your husband the other day. He was very welcoming."

Susan's face turned pale, and a look of disbelief etched into her wrinkles. "You what?"

"Doug? I met doug a few weeks ago when we moved in. Don't worry, he got in lots of walking that day, I can vouche for that," she chuckled. However, Susan's face just grew more horrified.

"Are you ok Susan? Did I say something wrong?"

"You met my Doug?"

"Yes?"

"That's impossible."

Carrie started getting uneasily nervous. "Why is that impossible?"

"Doug died a year ago in a car accident. Right outside your house actually. He had a heart attack while driving, a little after midnight. Our oldest daughter had gone into labor a town over and he was in a rush to get there and take her to the hospital. He must have gotten his heart too worked up that he had a heart attack and crashed the car into a tree. They said he died instantly."

There was a lump. A lump that consumed her throat and made it nearly impossible to swallow, or respond.

No wonder the police had not found anything. The light was not real. Doug was reliving the moment he died, every night at 12:18am.

Carrie and Lily tried to stick out their stay in their new home, and even called in a psychic to try to cleanse the energy on the property. However, every night at the same time, the headlights went on for a minute or two.

Doug never appeared to them again. The one welcoming conversation had been the one and only time they saw him. It became impossible to enjoy their new house with the activity occuring each night. More important, there did not appear to be any way to rid of it, They quickly relisted their home.

Doppelganger

After moving into a new house, expecting their first child, Drew and Mackenzie made the decision to adopt a dog from the local shelter.

Mackenzie was about five months pregnant at the time. Amid the morning sickness and slight stress of a first pregnancy, she was elated to welcome a furry friend into the family, as well as her child to-be.

Once at the shelter, they looked in all the cages, noting each one of those sad, pleading eyes. So many beautiful dogs needed homes and it was heart-breaking. While looking at the last row of dogs, an employee came up to them.

"This one is Boxer." She smiled and held her hand out to the Golden Retriever. He licked it immediately and wagged his tail. "He came in with his brother, who just got adopted."

Mackenzie grinned, "Oh that's wonderful his brother found a home." She leaned down and put her hand up to the cage as well, and Boxer licked her hand excitedly. His golden-haired tail wagged with delight.

"Oh, he is a very sweet boy," Drew chuckled, "He likes you Kenz!"

"I see that," she boasted proudly. "Do you think he could be the one?"

Drew nodded empathically. "I sure do."

"Well, just so you are aware," the employee explained, "Boxer and his brother had it a little rough. They came from a home where they were being mistreated and abused for several years. He is a sweetheart, but he might be a little withdrawn at first because of past experiences."

Mackenzie and Drew loved Boxer even more after hearing of his terrible start to life and adopted him immediately.

Once at home, Mackenzie was setting out Boxer's bowls and a few toys they had picked out before heading to the shelter. Boxer stood at her feet, displaying a few timid wags of his tail.

"You are such a sweet boy, Boxer," she patted his head, "Now, are you hungry?"

Boxer's tail went faster.

"Okay then, I will get something in this bowl for you!" She turned and placed the bowl on the kitchen counter while she opened the bag of dog food. Out of the corner of her eye, she saw something in the yard from the window.

She stopped what she was doing momentarily, and peered out the kitchen window. She could swear she was staring at Boxer in her yard.

Confused, Mackenzie turned around to find the dog at her feet, still expectantly waiting for his chow.

Now in a slight panic, she turned back towards the window. The dog that she had seen outside was no longer there.

She went back to opening the dog food bag and put the weird occurance out of her mind. She wanted to tell Drew, but he would probably tell her it was a trick of her mind, or pregancy hormones getting the best of her.

It was the first week of fall. The trees had begun their colorful decent to dormancy, the air had chilled, and it was time for Mackenzie to dig through her closet and pull out her winter wear.

It was the weekend and she could hear the neighbor kids giggling and enjoying jumping in piles of freshly fallen leaves from her bedroom window.

Boxer laid at the foot of her bed half asleep, seemingly enjoying just being in her company while she did her chores.

Box after box, she picked through items. This one will fit, this one won't, oh my gosh I forgotten I had that one, and Ewww what was I thinking even owning this one. Pretty much, that was the jist of it over and over for about an hour. Until… Boxer began whimpering in his sleep.

Mackenzie peeked over at him a ran a hand over his head to help calm him from the dream. Boxer stirred, but did not open his eyes.

She went back to hanging her fall clothing in her closet.

From downstairs, she heard a clang as if a bowl had fallen off of the counter. She furrowed her brow and listened further. Nothing.

She peered over at Boxer again, who normally would be awake and listening, but he was snoozing away. Weird.

She set the shirt she was in the middle of hanging on her dresser and went down stairs to investigate.

From the bottom of the stairs she could see the bowl in question on the floor. Before leaving her position on the bottom stair, she listened. Nothing. Still weird.

Finally, feeling everything was safe, she made her way light-footed to the kitchen and retrieved the bowl. Mackenzie turned it over in her hands checking for cracks, but it looked fine. Not a scratch on the darned thing.

Just as she was putting it away in the cupboard, she heard a low growl coming from the other side of the island.

Cautiously, she peered over the top of the counter at the floor on the other side. It was Boxer. He was looking up at her, teeth exposed and growling.

Panicing and shrieking, she tried her hardest to pull herself up on top of the island counter.

Once she had herself fully up there, she rocked herself back and forth, her eyes tightly shut.

After a few minutes of silence, she nervously opened one eye and peered down at the floor. Boxer was no longer there. What had gotten into him?

Uneasily, she retreated from the island counter and half ran back up the stairs to her room, terrified and perplexed.

Once inside the doorway of her bedroom, she quickly shut the door behind her and scanned the room for her cell phone. She needed to call Drew. She did not feel safe in this house alone right now.

Upon looking for her phone, her eyes settled upon the sleeping dog at the foot of her bed. Her jaw almost dropped right off of her face. Has he been there the whole time? What was going on with this dog?

The next morning she had phoned Drew. Drew had suggested she call her sister Charity and ask to stay the night with her. She ended the call filled with frustration. Mackenzie could tell that Drew did not quite believe her. To be honest, the more time that passed, the more the whole event had felt unreal.

Boxer was being an absolute angel, and there had been no more sightings of a twin dog. Maybe her mind was just playing tricks on her.

Mackenzie went into the kitchen and brewed a pot of coffee. She re-ran the events through her mind. Everything about the night before had felt so real. The dog had looked exactly like Boxer. It sounded exactly like him too.

She poured herself a cup of coffee and sat at the table. She swiped through the morning news on her ipad while she sipped at her drink.

Boxer mosied into the kitchen, with a couple long stretches of his hind legs mid-walk. He pranced to her feet and looked up at her with eyes that smiled "good morning" and sat comfortably at her feet.

The baby came in August. She was the light of their lives besides Boxer. Boxer too had become a cherished member of their family.

Mackenzie did not see the "other" Boxer for quite awhile until their baby girl Amber was two.

Mackenzie hinted some gloom in Boxer's eyes once bedtime came. He'd follow her into Amber's room and listen as she read her daughter a bedtime story. Then he would slowly amble out of the room after Mackenzie, always making sure to give Amber a generous amount of bedtime kisses before leaving.

It was a stormy night and Amber was fast asleep in her toddler bed. Mackenzie was in the living room watching a television show with the baby monitor on the coffee table and Boxer laying at her feet.

Drew was out of town again on business, so she had the house mostly to herself.

As the show ended, Mackenzie began folding her blanket up and turning off the lights. As she went to grab the baby monitor, she could hear growling over the device. One quick glance down told her that Boxer was still there at her side.

Her heart racing, she bolted towards her daughter's room. She stumbled in the dark to reach the stairs as fast as she could.

The stairs were a blur. All she could think of was Amber while taking them two at a time. Breathless, she reached Amber's room.

All was silent and serene. Lights danced on the walls from Amber's mobile. That was it. She scanned the room multiple times. Nothing.

Mackenzie silently closed the door and leaned her back against it. Was this the dog from a few years ago returning, or was she just tired and hearing things? After all, nothing had happened for quite a long time now.

She tucked herself into bed and read for awhile to shut her mind off.

The next day, Mackenzie was watching Amber playing with Boxer in the yard. Amber giggled as she fumbled over the grass to slowly chase the dog. She would get to him and give him a big hug and he'd lick her milky white cheek, then run a few steps ahead again and wait for her to catch him.

Boxer loved this game, and he loved Amber. The two were inseparable during the day.

"Drink!" Amber called to her mom. "Drink, drink, drink!"

Mackenzie waltzed over to her daughter and gave her a big kiss on the cheek. "Ok honey. Do you want juice, or milk?"

"Milky."

Her mother nodded, "Ok, I will be right back."

Amber giggled and continued playing with Boxer.

Jogging, Mackenzie ducked inside from the porch door and quickly grabbed a small milk box from the fridge, hurrying back outside.

Once outside and scanning the yard, she instantly dropped the milk box. It thudded on the back porch planks. Where was her daughter? She was just there!

Frantically calling for Amber, Mackenzie ran towards the trees that lined their backyard and bordered the highway.

Then Boxer appeared. He seemed to be frenzied as well, darting back and forth as if searching for his friend.

Mackenzie ran towards the back of the trees with a lump in her throat and tears stinging her eyes. That is when she saw it. A flash of blue from the road. Amber's shirt was blue!

"Amber!!!" Mackenzie called in a violent alarming shriek.

She had reached the road in time to see a long haul headed right towards her daughter.

In disbelief, she watched Boxer run out onto the road and knock Amber just far enough out of the way of the truck. However, he did not miss getting hit.

Mackenzie screamed in horror as her beloved pet took the blunt force of the vehicle.

The dog lay on the road, unmoving and clearly mortally injured.

Amber cried, "Mommy! Boxer hurt! Mommy!"

She shielded Amber's face from the scene at the road and carried her back to the house.

Mackenzie quickly called her neighbor and asked if he would help by removing Boxer from the road until she could figure out the next steps.

It took about fifteen minutes, but Mackenzie managed to get Amber calmed down enough to get her laid down for a nap.

A few minutes later her phone rang, her neighbor giving her an update. "Hey Kenz, I don't know how to tell you this, but... there is no dog out there on the road."

Mackenzie furrowed her brow, "What do you mean Bud? He was just there less than twenty minutes ago."

"Well I searched up and down the road a bit but there was no dog."

She wasn't sure if she was confused or horrified. "Ok... thanks anyways Bud."

Mackenzie hung up the phone, unsure of what to do next. Should she take the monitor with her and go look for the dog herself?

Just as she was opening the sliding glass door to go look for herself, she saw Boxer. He was sitting at the door waiting patiently to be let in, not a scratch on him.

Her jaw just about dropped right off of her face. He slid past her through the half open door and into the house. She stared after him in disbelief. How had he not been hit? What was happening?

After Boxer entered through the doorway past her and, as she looked up before shutting it, she spied the other dog in the distance. It seemed impossible, but he looked identical to Boxer. He was sitting like a sentinel at the edge of the trees, still covered in blood.

Their eyes met, and for a few moments, the two just connected. The dog eventually stood, and in the midst of limping off, just evaporated into nothing.

Mackenzie could not believe her eyes. What had just happened? Had some ghost dog or doppelganger of her dog just saved her daughter's life? She wiped tears from her cheek as she slowly shut the door.

FROM THE AUTHOR:

I have had a few ghost experiences. I've always believed & been curious since I was a child.

I used to wake when I was about four years old around 2-3 am often. I don't know how I knew, but I would get up and walk outside in the hallway. I would see what looked like dust particles form a sort of apparition and float down the hallway to my parent's room. Which would always disappear outside their door. Then I would go lay back down.

I never knew how & why this happened. And honestly the older I got I wondered how I was so fearless and didn't hide under my covers instead of following it.

That is my youngest event. I also saw my grandfather after he passed when I was about 7. Then, a few crazier ones as an adult.

One house horrified me to the point I had to be medicated because I was terrified to sleep at all.

Now I'm a writer of the paranormal. Maybe these experiences shaped me into who I am today. But I've always been sensitive. Am I psychic? Hell no.

But I get feelings. I feel dread, and something bad 80% of the time happens within a day.

I can usually walk into anyone's home and just know if something is off. When I moved into this house that haunted me, I knew. Something was off. Wasn't sure what. Didn't take me long before I figured it out though.

Follow Eve S. Evans on instagram
@eves.evansauthor

https://www.instagram.com/eves.evansauthor/

BOOKS BY EVE S. EVANS:

Printed in Great Britain
by Amazon